# Great Stories of
# Mystery
# and
# Suspense

# Great Stories of
# Mystery
# and
# Suspense

Selected and condensed by the editors of
**The Reader's Digest**

The Reader's Digest Association
Pleasantville, New York
Montreal, Sydney, Cape Town, Hong Kong

CONTENTS

**7**
## A Kiss Before Dying
by Ira Levin

**151**
## The King of the Rainy Country
by Nicolas Freeling

**255**
## Five Passengers From Lisbon
by Mignon G. Eberhart

**379**
## The Moving Target
by Ross Macdonald

**503**
## Strangers on a Train
by Patricia Highsmith

# A Kiss
# Before Dying

A CONDENSATION OF
THE BOOK BY

## Ira
## Levin

ILLUSTRATED BY JIM SHARPE

Dorothy . . . Ellen . . . Marion . . . the three daughters of Leo Kingship, copper magnate. Three pretty, intelligent young women with lots of money, and more to come when the old man is gone. Three natural targets for a cold-blooded fortune hunter.

But Dorothy spoils everything by getting pregnant, and she must go. Ellen comes too close to the truth about her sister's "suicide," so she too must die. Now it's Marion's turn . . . but the whole thing is preposterous. There's nothing amiss with Marion's fiancé, nothing that Kingship can quite put his finger on anyway. . . .

A shattering, spellbinding first novel from the author who went on to write *Rosemary's Baby* and *The Boys from Brazil*.

## One: Dorothy

His plans had been running so beautifully, so damned beautifully, and now *she* was going to smash them all. Hate erupted and flooded through him, gripping his face with jaw-aching pressure. That was all right, though; the lights were out.

She kept on sobbing weakly in the dark, her cheek pressed against his bare chest, her tears and her breath burning hot. He wanted to push her away.

Finally his face relaxed. His legs were quivering the way they always did when things took a crazy turn and caught him unprepared. He lay still for a moment, waiting for the trembling to subside, then he put his arm around her and stroked her back. With his free hand he drew the blanket up around her shoulders. "Crying isn't going to do any good," he told her gently.

Obediently, she tried to stop, rubbing her eyes with the worn binding of the blanket and catching her breath in long choking gasps. "It's just . . . the holding it in for so long. I've known for weeks. I didn't want to say anything until I was sure."

His hand on her back was warm. "No mistake possible?"

"No."

"How far?"

"Two months almost." She lifted her cheek from his chest. "What are we going to do?" she asked.

"You didn't give the doctor your right name, did you?"

"No. He knew I was lying though. It was awful."

"If your father ever finds out . . ."

She lowered her head again and repeated the question. "What are we going to do?"

"Listen, Dorrie," he said. "I know you want me to say we'll get married right away—tomorrow. And I want to marry you. More than anything else in the world." He paused, planning his words with care. "But if we marry this way, me not even meeting your father first, and then a baby comes seven months later . . . You know what he'd do."

"He couldn't *do* anything," she protested. "I'm over eighteen. Eighteen's all you have to be out here. What could he do?"

"I'm not talking about an annulment or anything like that."

"Then what? What do you mean?" she appealed.

"The money," he said. "Dorrie, what about him—him and his holy morals? Your mother makes a single slip; he finds out about it eight years later and divorces her, not caring about you and your sisters, not caring about her bad health. Well, what do you think he would do to you? He'd forget you ever existed. You wouldn't see a penny."

"I don't *care*," she said earnestly. "Do you think I care?"

"But I do, Dorrie." His hand began moving gently on her back again. "Not for me, but for you. What will happen to us? We'll both have to quit school; you for the baby, me to work. And what will I be? A clerk? Or an oiler in some textile mill or something? Living in a furnished room with paper drapes?"

"It doesn't matter."

"It does! You're only nineteen and you've had money all your life. You don't know what it means not to have it. I do. We'd be at each other's throats in a year."

She began sobbing again.

He closed his eyes and spoke dreamily. "I had it planned so beautifully. I would have come to New York this summer. I